Dear Parents:

Congratulations! Your child is taking the first steps on an exciting journey. The destination? Independent reading!

STEP INTO READING® will help your child get there. The program offers five steps to reading success. Each step includes fun stories and colorful art or photographs. In addition to original fiction and books with favorite characters, there are Step into Reading Non-Fiction Readers, Phonics Readers and Boxed Sets, Sticker Readers, and Comic Readers—a complete literacy program with something to interest every child.

Learning to Read, Step by Step!

Ready to Read   Preschool–Kindergarten
• big type and easy words • rhyme and rhythm • picture clues
For children who know the alphabet and are eager to begin reading.

Reading with Help   Preschool–Grade 1
• basic vocabulary • short sentences • simple stories
For children who recognize familiar words and sound out new words with help.

Reading on Your Own   Grades 1–3
• engaging characters • easy-to-follow plots • popular topics
For children who are ready to read on their own.

Reading Paragraphs   Grades 2–3
• challenging vocabulary • short paragraphs • exciting stories
For newly independent readers who read simple sentences with confidence.

Ready for Chapters   Grades 2–4
• chapters • longer paragraphs • full-color art
For children who want to take the plunge into chapter books but still like colorful pictures.

STEP INTO READING® is designed to give every child a successful reading experience. The grade levels are only guides; children will progress through the steps at their own speed, developing confidence in their reading.

Remember, a lifetime love of reading starts with a single step!

Visit us on the Web!
StepIntoReading.com
randomhouse.com/kids

Educators and librarians, for a variety of teaching tools, visit us at
RHTeachersLibrarians.com

ISBN 978-0-7364-3240-5 (trade) — ISBN 978-0-7364-8153-3 (lib.bdg.)
ISBN 978-0-7364-3241-2 (ebook)

Printed in the United States of America
10 9 8 7 6 5 4 3 2 1

STEP 2 STEP READING WITH HELP

STEP INTO READING®

BRAVE FIREFIGHTERS

By Apple Jordan
Illustrated by the Disney Storybook Art Team

Random House 🏠 New York

Dusty is a racing champ!
He lives in
Propwash Junction.

Dusty races
his friend Skipper.
Something is wrong.
Dusty spins
out of control!

Dusty's engine is broken.

He cannot fly fast.

Dottie cannot fix him.

Dusty wants to race.

He tries again.

He crashes!

The crash starts a fire.
Dusty's friends
help put it out.
Everyone cheers!

Mayday is
a firefighter.

Dusty wants to be

a firefighter, too!

Dusty goes
to Piston Peak
Air Attack Base.

He meets other
firefighters there.

Blade is
the best firefighter.
He puts out fires fast!
Dusty wants
to be like him.

Dusty trains.
It is hard
to fight fires!

The next day,
there is a forest fire.
Dusty helps
the other firefighters.
He puts
out the fire.

Dusty goes
to a party
at the lodge.

He greets the guests.

They are happy

to meet a famous racer.

The next morning,
there are more fires.
Dusty flies in
to help.

Flames are getting close
to the lodge.

The guests must leave!

Dusty falls
into the river.
He needs help!

Blade flies in
and saves Dusty.

Blade and Dusty hide
from the fire.

The fire is spreading.

It is blocking the road.

The guests need help!

Dusty and the firefighters
work together.
They put
out the fire!

The road is clear.
The guests can drive
out of the park.
They are safe!

Dusty puts out
another fire.
It is on a bridge.
He saves more guests!

Dusty flies too fast.

His engine stops.

He crashes!

Dusty wakes up.
His friends
have fixed him!
Dusty is done
with his training.

Dusty flies home.

He is

a brave firefighter!